HERODOTUS
and the Road to History

by JEANNE BENDICK

Pictures by the author

Bethlehem Books • Ignatius Press
Bathgate   San Francisco

Cover art by Jeanne Bendick
Cover design by Marie Leininger

First printing September 2009

ISBN: 978-1-932350-20-3
Library of Congress Control Number: 2009931271

Bethlehem Books • Ignatius Press
10194 Garfield Street South
Bathgate, ND 58216
www.bethlehembooks.com
1-800-757-6831

Printed in the United States on acid-free paper

Contents

Author's Preface

Herodotus was born 2,500 years ago in the Greek town of Halicarnassus, on the Asian coast of what is now Turkey. He lived in a time in Greece when myth and legend, told in song and poetry, were considered history. But there was no Greek word for "history," as we define it now—a record of the human past.

As far as we know, Herodotus wrote the first such record of this kind springing from the pure thirst for knowledge. It was not only the first history, it was the first long work in prose—ordinary language. (The Greeks did not even have a word for prose.) Herodotus described his writing as a *historie*, which was the Greek word for "inquiry"—which means "finding out."

You could call "finding out" the theme of Herodotus' life. He had a fever for inquiring that was unique, even among the always-curious Greeks. He wanted to see things for himself, even if it meant going to the ends of the known earth.

To put myself in Herodotus' sandals, I had to become a detective. Most of what we know about his inquiries and his travels comes from his own writing, his Histories. But what about the everyday world he lived in? What was it like to be a Greek in the fifth century BC? Even Herodotus, an extraordinary Greek, lived in a day-to-day world.

What did he do when he was growing up? What did he study? What did he eat and what did he wear? What was his house like, and his town?

What did he look like? What did the people he wrote about look like?

What made him set out to explore his world?

I have drawn a number of maps so you can follow Herodotus in his travels and in the history he describes. They also let you compare his places with our world today. Over all these centuries the places are the same, though they may have different names. I have used modern place names, but a page at the back of the book shows you what those places were called in Herodotus' time.

(When speaking as Herodotus, I have also used modern measurements instead of the ones used in his time. You can compare those at the back of the book, too.)

Traveling in Herodotus' time was difficult and dangerous. Usually he went by boat, but what were the boats like? Was a boat on the Nile different from a Phoenician trader?

Of course, putting myself in Herodotus' sandals took guesswork and imagination, but it also took research. Ancient Greek paintings and pottery show and tell vivid stories; so do portraits and sculptures of the people Herodotus wrote about.

The ancient Egyptians painted pictures of their lives and told about them in symbols called hieroglyphs. The Persians carved pictures of triumphs and described them in their own cuneiform writing.

Over the hundred generations since Herodotus lived, archaeologists have slowly discovered and recovered much of what we know now about the world he lived in. And many historians after him have added their own pieces to the puzzle. Using many sources, I have imagined a particular life 2,500 years ago.

Herodotus was a person of his own time. He wasn't every person, though. Herodotus was unique, doing something no one had ever done before. He was looking for a new way to explain the nature of things and to record his ideas about why they happened. And he wrote it all down!

Jeanne Bendick

Guilford, Connecticut
July 2009

1

I Am Herodotus

MY NAME is Herodotus. (Ha-ROD-ah-tus.)

Some people call me the Father of History.

Some people call me the World's Greatest Traveler.

Some unkind people call me the Father of Lies, but they haven't been to all the places I have been, or seen all the sights I have seen, or listened to all the stories I have heard.

484 B.C. I am a Greek, born in the city-state of Halicarnassus (Hol-li-kar-NASS-us) at the edge of the Mediterranean Sea. A city-state is

1

just what it sounds like—a city that rules itself and the lands around it.

Halicarnassus is on the Asian shore of the sea, and when I was born it had been part of the Persian Empire for sixty years. That didn't matter to us; we still considered ourselves Greeks.

ANCIENT GREECE

The Greeks were scattered all around the Mediterranean Sea. We Ionian Greeks lived on the Asian shore and on islands along that shore. There were other Greek city-states such as Thebes

2

and Corinth, Athens and Sparta, on the European mainland. We lived around our sea like frogs around a pond.

We weren't really a nation at all—just a collection of scattered city-states. Some were small, some bigger and more powerful, each making its own laws and ruling itself in its own way. Each city-state considered itself superior to the others and there was quarreling—even war—among us.

We were cut off from one another by water or by mountains. Still, we all spoke the same language, worshiped the same gods and kept the same customs. We were all Greeks. People who were not Greeks were considered barbarians.

The Persian Empire was the greatest power in the world. It stretched across Asia to India in the east; across Europe to Italy in the west; from the Black Sea in the north, across the Mediterranean Sea to Egypt in the south. Still, we scattered Greeks managed to defeat the mighty Persians.

How did we do that? I'll tell you how we did it, but that's only part of my story. Let's begin at the beginning.

SCYTHIANS
SEA OF AZOV DON R. VOLGA R. URAL R. SCYTHIANS
THRACE
DANUBE R. BLACK SEA ARAL SEA
CASPIAN SEA
ARMENIA BACTRIA
LYDIA MEDIA PARTHIA
TIGRIS R.
MEDITERRANEAN SEA PHOENICIA EUPHRATES R. BABYLON
LIBYA PERSIA
EGYPT
NILE R. ARABIA INDIA
ANCIENT GREECE RED SEA
IONIA

THE PERSIAN EMPIRE

RUSSIA
UKRAINE VOLGA R. URAL R. KAZAKHSTAN
ROMANIA ARAL SEA
DANUBE R. BLACK SEA CASPIAN SEA UZBEKISTAN
BULGARIA TURKMENISTAN
GREECE TURKEY
MEDITERRANEAN SYRIA TIGRIS R. AFGHANISTAN
SEA LEBANON EUPHRATES R. IRAN
ISRAEL IRAQ
LIBYA EGYPT JORDAN PAKISTAN
NILE R. SAUDI ARABIA PERSIAN GULF
RED SEA

THE AREA TODAY

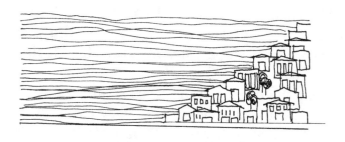

2

I Grow Up

HALICARNASSUS WAS a busy and interesting place to grow up in. People from other Greek city-states lived there. So did Persians from around the empire and traders from all around the Mediterranean Sea. When I was growing up, it seemed the center of the world.

Halicarnassus is shaped like half a giant soup bowl. At the bottom of the bowl is the harbor, crowded with ships from all over the Mediterranean Sea.

Near the harbor is the agora—the giant market where food and goods from everywhere are sold and traded. The theaters, the law courts and other gathering places are here, too.

Rising up around the bowl of the hill are peoples' houses. Poor people, tradesmen and craftsmen live toward the bottom. Rich and important people live higher on the hill.

My parents, Lyxes and Dryo, were part of one of those important families. My cousin, Panyasis, was a famous poet and we were close in family relationship to Artemisia, the tyrant of Halicarnussus. ("Tyrant" is our way of saying "all-powerful ruler.")

Artemisia was also famous, because she was the woman commander of a Persian ship during the wars. Artemisia came home from the wars when I was about four years old.

When I was very young I spent most of my time with my mother and the family's slaves. We Greeks and Persians really depend on our slaves. Some are prisoners, captured in wars or by pirates. Some are people who cannot pay their debts. Some are the children of slaves.

Our slaves are civil servants and teachers. (I know for sure that many captured slaves are better educated than their masters.) Slaves run our households, do the cooking and the laundry. Some are artisans and some keep the peace. Some are even soldiers. Of course, many are the laborers who clean up, build roads and houses and work in the mines.

As I grew up, I had my own slave who took care of my clothes, looked after my safety, taught me manners and how to behave like a proper Greek.

We Greek people live simply, even the rich ones. We have contempt for the sumptuous lifestyle of the Persians, even though we are somewhat fascinated by it.

Our houses aren't big and they don't have a lot of furniture. We have plain chairs, and low tables for eating. My bed was a couch in the daytime and there are no cupboards or closets—we fold our clothes and linen into wooden chests.

When I got dressed in the morning I put on my chiton, (KY-ten) a squarish cloth with holes for the head and arms. If it was cold, I wore a cloak over my chiton. Had I been poor, my cloak would be my blanket at night.

We Greeks eat simply—barley bread and olives, fruit, beans and cheese, sometimes fish and rarely, meat. For something sweet, we use honey. Sometimes we drink goats' milk. Usually, we drink water, or water mixed with wine.

Slaves draw the water from a well, or bring it in jars from a public fountain. Could a house ever

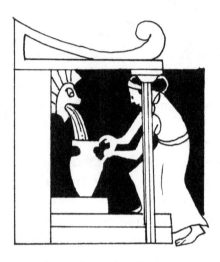

have a water supply inside? What a dream! But we did have a room with a bathtub which a slave filled with heated water. And we had a cooking room with a grill where slaves did the cooking. That grill gave us some heat when it was cold.

The Persians think the Greek way of life is odd. They love rich foods and ornaments, pomp and splendor. They think they have earned it by conquering their world.

As I got older, when I went to school (from sunrise to sunset,) I learned the letters of the Greek alphabet and the letters of the cuneiform (KYOO-nee-i-form) alphabet that the Persians used. At

THE GREEK ALPHABET

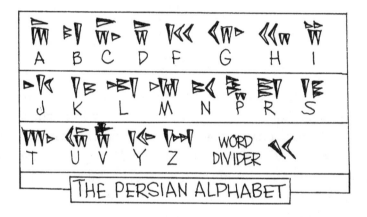

THE PERSIAN ALPHABET

first we wrote with a stylus, on a wax-covered tablet. When we became better writers, we wrote in ink on papyrus, a paper imported from Egypt.

We listened as our teachers sang and recited the works of Homer, which told of great wars, long past. I learned the Iliad and the Odyssey by heart, but I wondered if those things had really happened or if they were only stories. I often thought about that.

9

Our wars with the Persians seemed much more real—of course, they were recent, when some of our Greek city-states began a revolt against the Persians. When I was six, the European Greeks had defeated the Persian Emperor, Xerxes, (ZERK-seez) on the mainland. We cheered their victory, but the Persians were still overlords here in Halicarnassus.

We recited our lessons to music and we learned to dance, to play the lyre and the pipes, to speak well, and to argue. Debating is a big part of being an educated Greek.

We studied astronomy and geometry, but I particularly liked geography. Our Greek geographers were wonderful. First there was Anaximander, (An-ax-i-MAN-der) of Miletus who, more

10

than a hundred years ago, had made a map of the world surrounded by Ocean. How did he know that?

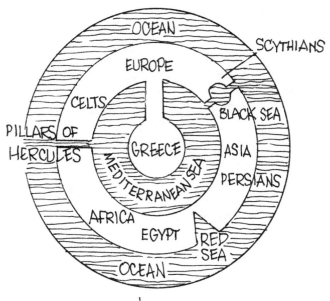

ANAXIMANDER'S MAP OF THE WORLD

And then there was Hecataeus, (Ha-KAY-tee-us) also from Miletus, who had recently traveled our world himself. His world map was a real improvement on Anaximander's, and he made other, more detailed maps.

What wonders had he seen? Had he actually been to all those places? What were the plants and animals like? How did the people live? I had so many questions that didn't have answers.

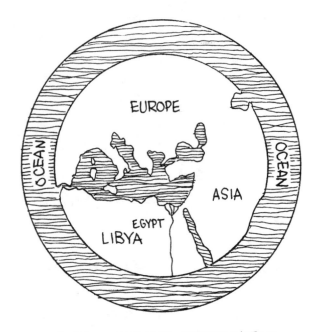

HECATAEUS' MAP OF THE WORLD

Sports weren't my favorite, but they were an important part of our school day. They were outside, in the palaestra (pal-ES-tra.) We ran and we jumped, we wrestled and boxed, we shot arrows and flung disks.

And we learned the art of war, even how to be a soldier. Our Greek soldiers are called hoplites. Some of us served in the army for two years when we finished school.

If you were rich, life in Halicarnassus was good. Men spent most of their time outside the house. (Women never went out alone, only with their slaves or with women friends and relatives.)

Men usually did the shopping along with their slaves, mingling with the crowds at the agora. They talked politics and philosophy and argued with their friends. They went to the theater, listened to public speakers and went to the law courts to hear cases.

As I grew up, at first I did all the things the other men did, but I was restless and uneasy. What I really liked was to go down to the harbor and roam around the boats that came and went from all over the Mediterranean Sea. The sights and smells, the sails and masts, the sense of adventure excited me.

I listened to the stories the traders told, about Egypt and Persia and the Greek mainland, and about caravans from mysterious places where there were strange people, even monsters. I listened to the tales of sailors

who rowed the triremes (TRI-reems)—the Greek warships. The traders were independent business-men. The rowers were full-time professionals—the best-paid workers in Greece.

I was still in Halicarnassus, but now it seemed too small. It seemed more of an outpost than the center of the world.

3

My Travels Begin

IN HALICARNASSUS, a revolt was brewing. First, Artemisia, and then her son had died. Now Lygdamis, Artemisia's grandson, was tyrant. He was cruel and iron-handed. Most of us hated him.

We talked about the Greek colonies along the coast of the Aegean Sea that had fought and defeated their Persian rulers to become independent city-states. Why couldn't Halicarnassus do that too? So we held secret meetings and made plans for an uprising against Lygdamis. My family was deeply involved in the plot.

But Lygdamis got wind of the planned uprising. He punished the plotters and sent my family into exile, with orders to stay away from Halicarnassus.

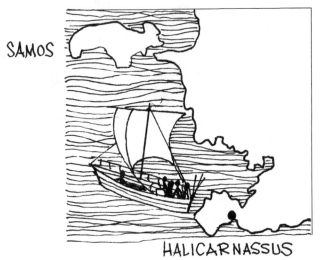

SAMOS

HALICARNASSUS

With our slaves and our possessions crowded onto a small cargo ship, we sailed north along the coast of Asia Minor to the island of Samos, which had freed itself from Persian rule some years before. Maybe there was something about Samos that encouraged famous people. The great Greek mathematician, Pythagoras, had lived there. So did the slave, Aesop. He was the one who wrote the Fables.

Samos was bigger than Halicarnassus and a center of culture, but it didn't satisfy me either. Again, I took to wandering around the waterfront.

Look where Samos is.

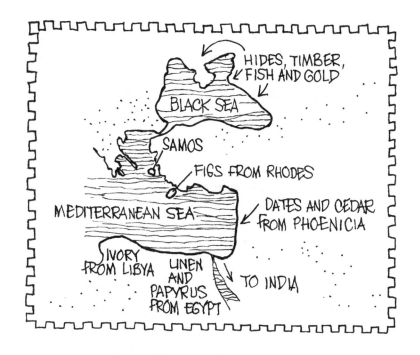

It's just in the right place to be a trading center for goods from all over the Mediterranean Sea. It's close enough to the mainland to connect it with the trade routes to the north and into Asia. Some ships even sailed all the way to India, and came back loaded with spices, tortoiseshell and pearls.

I asked, but I never found anyone who could give me firsthand information about the existence of a sea beyond Europe, to the north and west, even though Anaximander and Hecataeus showed Ocean there. Still, tin and amber do come to us from what one may call the ends of the earth.

I watched the boats loading wine and honey, olives and pottery, to trade. (Samos is famous for its pottery.) I watched boats coming in from the mysterious north, unloading hides and timber, mackerel and other fish, even gold. I watched them unloading sacks of grain, great rolls of papyrus and linen cloth from Egypt, raisins and figs from Rhodes, dates and cedar logs from Phoenicia and ivory from Libya.

The docks were piled with sacks of all sizes, with jars of wine and oil, piles of dried fish, bales of papyrus cloth, coils of rope, baskets of dried fruit, and crowded with loaders and unloaders laughing and shouting in some languages I had never heard.

I walked around the docks, talking to the traders who spoke Greek, asking about their travels. At first, the traders were suspicious of me. Why would I want to make friends with them? Traders weren't considered important, even though they were.

But I was eager to listen to their adventures and had stories of my own to trade with them— myths and tales they had never heard. After a while they accepted me as one of them.

It became clear to me what I wanted to do—to travel, not as a trader but as an explorer, even a kind of scientist, asking questions and collecting information. I wanted to see the world for myself as Hecataeus the mapmaker had, maybe to see even more. Should I accept another man's view of the world?

Of course there were problems that I would have to figure out.

I spoke only Greek. Could I find translators who spoke both Greek and the barbarian languages?

I could carry rolls of papyrus to write things down, but I could also depend on my excellent memory, thanks to all that training on Homer's poetry.

I would have to find ships and traders going where I wanted to go, and I would certainly want to travel inland, but how could I travel when I'm not aboard ship? I don't find riding a horse comfortable, but maybe I could find a horse and cart. Probably, I would walk. We Greeks walk long distances.

Where to start my travels?

The north was mysterious. There didn't seem to be any real cities—at least, nobody talked about them. What kind of people lived there? The traders said they were savages—even cannibals, they whispered.

I could pay for my passage, so with the help of my trading friends I arranged to sail on a ship that was going north. The ship wasn't big—less than 30 paces long. It had a big, square sail hung from a mast in the middle of the boat. No oarsmen to help us when the wind wasn't blowing—only warships had oars and oarsmen. And there wasn't much deck—just a wide platform around the sides. The cargo was stored below, in the middle of the boat.

We sailed north along the Asian coast between

the islands and the mainland, keeping close to shore so the captain could see familiar landmarks. We did not sail at night.

So, saying goodbye to my friends and family, I began my travels, my inquiries and adventures. It would be years before I returned from this first great journey.

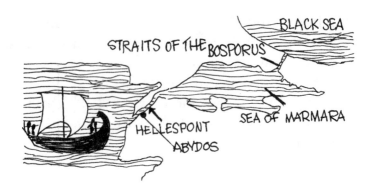

4

To the North

ON THIS STOUT little trading ship, I sailed north-east into the waters of the Hellespont, which separates Europe from Asia.

We stopped on the Asian shore in the city of Abydos, where I met a number of people who, years before, had watched the Persian king, Xerxes, building his bridges across the Hellespont so he could invade Europe. His father, Darius, hadn't managed to conquer the Greeks there, and Xerxes had been trying again. He was on his way to a big defeat.

At this point the Hellespont is about a mile wide. Xerxes' first two side-by-side bridges were held by enormous ropes that broke in a violent storm which carried the bridges away. Xerxes cut off the heads of the engineers who had built them and, in a rage against the Hellespont, ordered his soldiers to punish the water with a terrible beating, using whips. We Greeks still laugh at that.

New engineers built two more bridges, this time of ships lashed together. People told me how Xerxes sat on his marble throne to watch as his huge army, gathered from all over Asia, marched across. They said that one nation had furnished ships, another foot soldiers, a third supplied horses, others transports, ships and provisions. They said it took seven days and seven nights for all of them to cross into Europe.

It must have been a mighty spectacle. I looked for remains of those bridges but I could not find them.

We sailed north up the Hellespont and into the waters of the Sea of Marmara—not a big sea, but big enough and rough enough, so I was glad to see the straits of the Bosporus ahead.

Again, there were large, prosperous Greek towns on both shores. People told me that Darius had built a bridge of boats somewhere along here, too, but again, I could not find any signs of it.

At its far end, the Bosporus opens up into the Black Sea, which seemed to me bigger and more open than my part of the Mediterranean. We navigated from town to town along the European coast and since towns were not connected by any roads, I had a fine time exchanging news and gossip among them.

Then we were in Thrace, which I thought must be the largest nation in the world except for India. Still, all along the shore the cities were Greek. I wanted to travel inland, so I had to find experienced travelers or even to hire armed guards to go with me because it wasn't safe to go alone. It wasn't safe to sail along this part of the Black Sea coast, either! There were too many shallow, marshy places where pirates hid.

The main occupation of these Thracians along the shore is wrecking unsuspecting ships. Their only income is from plunder and they are scornful of people who work for a living. They also sell their children to traders. (I must admit that we Greeks buy them.) Some tribes are tattooed all over, which is marvelous to see.

Inland, I came across tribes living in a strange way on smaller lakes. They built their houses on platforms resting on piles driven into the lake bed. Families lived their whole lives on those platforms, fishing for their meals through trap doors. All the people and their animals lived on fish.

As we made our way back to the coast, I found the tribes more civilized—more Greek.

Sailing again, northeast along the coast, we came to the river Danube, which seemed to me to be the mightiest river in the world. North of the Danube the people have small, shaggy horses— too small to ride, but good at pulling carts and chariots. I did not travel much beyond the mouth of the river. I heard that there were so many bees there that travel was impossible. I like getting stung as little as the next man.

We sailed along the coast, east into Scythia, another land of majestic rivers. The rivers Bug and Dnieper flow into a great inlet where the Greek city of Olbia is. I was weary of traveling, so I made Olbia my headquarters for a long time, staying with a Greek family as a paying, guest friend.

The water here is sweet and the fish are excellent. There is one kind of enormous fish (sturgeon)— would you believe, weighing more than a thousand pounds—that people dry and use throughout the year.

I felt at home in Olbia. The people speak Greek, dress like Greeks and worship Apollo.

But the climate was nothing like Greece. The weather in the winter was terrible—bitterly cold, and the ground froze like iron. In summer there were many thunderstorms and a lot of rain. But I got to see a great deal while I was there.

The people around this part of the Black Sea are the most uncivilized on earth. These Scythians fight on horseback with bows and arrows and they live as nomads. They never plant crops, but are always moving their goods and families in carts, taking their cattle with them.

In this way, the wily Scythians had outwitted Darius years before. The Scythians rode toward the army of Darius with their best horsemen, but all the wagons in which the children and women lived they sent northward with all the cattle, (leaving only as much as they needed to supply themselves) and told the women to proceed continually toward the North Wind.

When the Persians saw the horsemen of the Scythians, the Persians came after them while the Scythians continually lured them on, and the Persians continued to pursue them. Now so long as the Persians were passing through Scythia they found nothing to eat, and nothing of the Scythians to destroy, seeing that the land was bare.

As I heard more about the people who lived farther inland, they seemed stranger and stranger.

I heard that some were absolutely bald, and ate only the fruit of one kind of tree, made into juice and mixed with milk. I heard that farther on, beyond the mountains, the people had goats' feet, and still farther away they slept for half the year. I heard

28

that some were Amazons, where the women ruled and fought the wars.

I heard that still farther north, the people had only one eye, and beyond them was a country where griffins guarded the gold. And that even beyond that, the people who live past Boreas, the North Wind, couldn't see where they were going because the cold air was so full of flying feathers.

Of course I didn't believe all these stories, but I couldn't go everywhere myself, so I did listen to people who claimed to be eyewitnesses.

I was told about the Caspian Sea, a sea not connected to any other sea, which I thought was strange. After all, the Aegean Sea is connected to the Mediterranean Sea which is connected to the Atlantic Ocean which joins the Indian Ocean, so most seas are really one big sea. Oddly, rivers flow into the Caspian but it seems to have no outlet.

I heard that this Caspian was so big that it was 15 days rowing in length and 8 days rowing wide. I have found that a good way to describe distances is by the time it takes to do something: as far as a boat can sail in 11 days, or as far as one can travel on foot in 14 days.

All along the coasts of the Black Sea and the Sea of Azov, and then all the way up the Don River, I met Greek traders doing a brisk business with the tribes there, trading our wares for furs and gold. Our vessel also did well.

When my ship returned to the Bosporus on its way home, I decided to make another trip in the

region while I had the chance, so I joined some
traders going by land to Colchis (KOL-kiss), at the
eastern end of the Black Sea. They told me that a
fast traveler could make the journey in 30 days.
But I wasn't in a hurry, so I didn't mind that we
took longer.

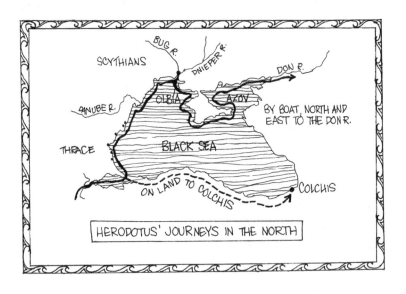

HERODOTUS' JOURNEYS IN THE NORTH

I remembered Colchis from my Homer. Homer
told how Jason went to Colchis in his ship, Argo,
which was supposed to be the first sea-going vessel. His crew was a band of heroes called the Argonauts.

Jason's mission was to get the precious Golden
Fleece, which had been stolen from his father. The
Colchis king, Aeetes, tried to prevent Jason from
getting the fleece, but Medea, the king's daughter,
helped him. Jason and Medea, with the fleece, fled
Colchis, back to Greece.

Homer says that years later, in revenge for the abduction of Medea, the Trojans abducted the Greek princess, Helen. I think that all this abducting was the beginning of the quarrels between the Greeks and the Persians—between Europe and Asia.

After seeing Colchis I decided it was finally time to go home to Samos. I had been away for eight or nine years!

5

Back to Samos and Away Again, to Babylon

WHEN I FINALLY got back to Samos after my years
of travels in the north, I found my family organiz-
ing a new assault on Halicarnassus, still trying
to get rid of the tyrant Lygdamis. (Stubbornness
certainly runs in our family.) This time we did it!

Lygdamis was overthrown and the family moved back to Halicarnassus, which was now Greek.

For some years, I was involved in the political affairs of the city, but again I grew more and more restless, wondering what was going on in the world outside and eager to continue my inquiries and explorations. I began wandering the waterfront again, talking to the traders, thinking about where to go next.

I most admired the Phoenicians, who I think are the best sailors in the world, with the best boats.

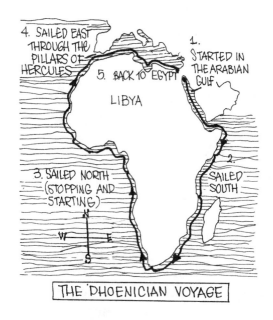

THE PHOENICIAN VOYAGE

I have heard a story about Phoenician sailors, who, more than a hundred years ago, sailed around the whole continent of Africa, which they

33

called Libya. They started south in the Arabian Gulf, sailed and stopped, sailed again, then sailed north, (so they said) and after three years sailed east through the Pillars of Hercules and back to Egypt.

I find it hard to believe that story, but the Phoenicians do dominate the Mediterranean and they sail to the edges of the known world. Of course,

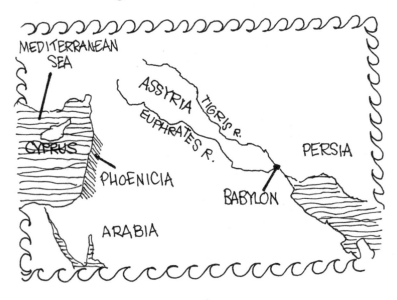

no one knows the extent of Europe, or of the great Ocean, but the Phoenicians sail even to the Tin Islands, somewhere in that Ocean to the north, trading glass and pottery, their famous cedar trees and the beautiful purple cloth they dye from murex seashells.

I decided to go to Phoenicia.

Phoenicia, like Greece, is a collection of city-states on a strip of land along the eastern shore of the Mediterranean.

It's on the way to everything farther east in Asia: Persia, Assyria, Arabia, even India. Phoenicia was under Persian rule at this time, and we Greeks were still at war with the Persians, but it wasn't an all-out, everywhere war, so I felt I could travel there safely. Besides, Phoenicia is full of Greeks and the people speak some mixture of Greek which would make it easier for me.

So my mind was made up. I chose a trader I liked, we reached an agreement, and I was off! Our ship sailed southeast, hugging the shore, past the great island of Cyprus, to land in the Phoenician colony of Myriandrus, in the Gulf of Issus.

What I wanted, first, was to see Babylon, which was quite a way inland.

On shore, a number of caravans were assembling,

loading goods from Phoenicia and from all over the Mediterranean to take inland. The caravans would divide at the great Euphrates River, some going north, some south, some beyond, into Asia.

Wares were loaded onto mules and camels and people were loaded onto horses for the slow, sandy, rocky trip, about 100 miles across the Syrian desert. Horses are not my favorite mode of transportation. On some days, I walked.

We traveled, too slowly for me, across Syria until we came to the great river, where I looked for a boat to take me downriver to Babylon. I was amazed to see leather cargo boats of many sizes, all as round as platters, floating down the river with the current. They had come all the way from Armenia in the north, with their wares.

With two men steering, each boat carried goods

and one or more donkeys to Babylon. I was told that when the cargo was sold, the boats were taken apart and the hides loaded onto the donkeys for the long, long walk upstream, where they were rebuilt for another trip downstream to market.

I didn't travel in one of those boats! I found a good little wooden cargo ship for my trip down the Euphrates. It was about 600 miles to Babylon.

For weeks we sailed through great fields of grain on both sides of the river. I thought they must be the richest in the world—enough to supply the whole Persian Empire. There was sesame growing,

too, which the captain said produced all the oil used in the country. I did not see any fruit trees or vines—no olives, no figs, no grapes. But there were date palms everywhere, which provided not only food, wine and honey, but also the fiber to make rope and baskets.

Since the climate is dry, the farmers constantly irrigate their fields with ingenious devices of rods

MY MAP OF BABYLON

FORTRESS

MOAT

WALL

PALACE AND
HANGING
GARDENS

MAIN GATE

GATE

OLD
CITY

NEW CITY

ZIGGURAT

CANAL

CANAL

MOAT

EUPHRATES R.

TEMPLE OF
MARDUK

HOUSES
AND
GARDENS

MOAT

MOAT

MOAT

THEY SAY THAT THE ZIGGURAT
WAS THE TOWER OF BABEL.

and buckets. We sailed past irrigation dikes and
past canals leading to other rivers. Finally, we
reached the Royal Canal which joins the Euphrates and the Tigris Rivers. Boats sail easily through
this canal from one great river into the other.

And then we came to Babylon.

It is surely the most enormous, most splendid
city in the world. The city is a great square, almost 14 miles on each side, surrounded by first, a
deep moat full of water. Next, there is a wall about
30 feet wide and about 120 feet high. There are

houses on the wall and room for four-horse chariots to drive abreast. I could not count the massive bronze gates in the wall.

About a hundred years ago the Persian King, Cyrus, laid siege to Babylon and finally took it over.

I was told that owing to the vast size of the place, long after the outer portions of the town were taken, the inhabitants of the central parts (as the residents of Babylon declare) knew nothing of what had chanced, but as they were engaged in a festival, continued dancing and reveling until they heard news of the capture.

About 50 years before Cyrus conquered the city, its king, Nebuchadnezzar, had captured Jerusalem and brought the Jews to Babylon. Cyrus freed them and sent them home.

The Euphrates flows right through the city and the river is lined with docks, crowded with trading ships. The houses are three and four stories tall and there is one tower that seems to scrape the sky. It is topped with glazed blue tiles and people tell me that this is the Tower of Babel.

Beside it is the great temple to the Babylonian god Marduk. I heard that when Cyrus came to Babylon there was a solid gold statue of Marduk in the temple, 15 feet high. Cyrus and later, Darius, respected the god and left it there, but Xerxes carried it away and melted it down.

I was in Babylon about 30 years after Xerxes. I saw so many things with my own eyes, and heard so many stories about past events that I stopped to write everything down.

Although its more glorious days are past, Babylon is still grand and beautiful, a hum of trade and business, alive with artists, astronomers and scientists.

6

I Go to Egypt

AFTER SOME TRAVELING and some time at home,
in about my 35th year I sailed to Egypt. I wanted
to observe with my own eyes this ancient civilization about which I had heard so much. There was
no way we could keep land in sight, so we sailed
by the stars. I stood at the raised helm with the
helmsman while the others slept, and he pointed
out for me the fixed stars and the ones that moved,
the wanderers.

About a day's sail away from land we began
to see more and more silt in the water, certainly

being washed out from the land. Then we sailed into the Nile Delta, where the great river flows into the Mediterranean Sea. This is called Lower Egypt because the Nile flows from the higher lands in the south down to the lower lands at the mouth of the river.

I was astonished at the soil there—rich, black as pitch, and I think it must be the most fertile in the world. Farms are everywhere, with wheat as the main crop. The farmers don't have to think about rain or irrigation—they just wait for their fields to be watered by the Nile as the river floods out of its banks every year. When the Nile floods, this whole part of Egypt becomes a great sea. Our boat didn't have to stay in the banks of the river at all.

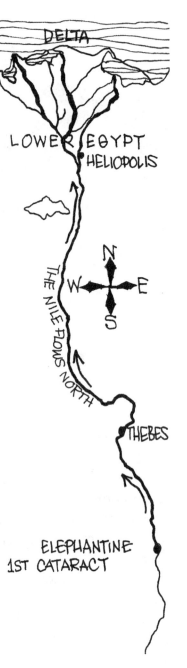

Why does the Nile flood only in the summer? I don't know. Where does the Nile come from? I don't know that, either. Hecataeus says it flows from the great Ocean, but I don't believe that. I am still trying to think of scientific explanations for those problems.

The Nile delta is crowded with cities. There must be 20,000 towns in Egypt. There are colonies from all over Greece, even from Halicarnassus, and they trade throughout the Mediterranean, as far as the Pillars of Hercules. There are also many Greek tourists who have come to marvel at what the Egyptians have built, long before our own history. I'm sure Hecataeus didn't come as a tourist. He was interested in deeper things.

The Egyptian people in their manners and customs seem to have reversed the ordinary practices

of mankind. The women go to market and take care of business, while many men are either priests or stay at home weaving. Of course there are many tradesmen and artisans of all sorts.

And they have doctors for every part of the body! In Greece, a doctor treats the whole body, but the Egyptians have doctors for eyes, heads, hearts, stomach, even teeth! They do seem very healthy but they have an unhealthy obsession with death.

Egyptian science must be the best anywhere. The Egyptians discovered the solar year, and they were the first to divide the year into 12 parts of 30 days each. And as I traveled around I was impressed by the way they used geometry for so many practical purposes. Everywhere I saw surveyors using instruments to measure the land. Their engineers have been using geometry for thousands of years to construct their enormous buildings.

Anyone would be amazed, gaping up at the pyramids which were built 2,000 years ago. But I think it must have exhausted the Egyptian people to build them. I cannot even calculate how many people, how much time and treasure that took.

The Egyptian kings certainly weren't afraid to take on grand projects. Many years ago, King Nechos II began to excavate a canal that would connect the Nile River to the Red Sea. Nechos never finished his canal, but years later Darius did and I saw the remains of that canal. The canal was wide enough so that two triremes could row there, side by side. Sailing from the Nile to the Red Sea took only four days, I heard—a fast way to get to the Red Sea and on to India.

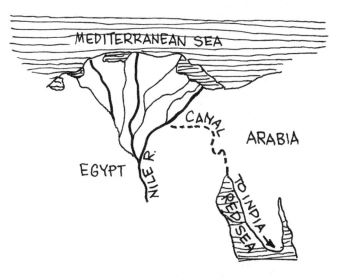

The canal has fallen into disuse. But the idea of a shortcut was a good one. Someone will surely try it again. Maybe there is a better place to build it.

In our sailing boat, which is different from any I have seen, we sailed on up the Nile. It is nine days'

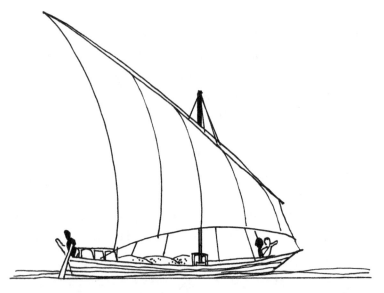

journey from Heliopolis, at the Delta, to Thebes, which, for ages, has been the capital of Egypt. The buildings and statues there are astonishing. I think that Thebes must be the oldest city in the world.

To prove how old their civilization is, the priests showed me statues of more than 300 generations of their ancestors. They were all human beings. (The Egyptians are amused that the Greeks believe, as I do, that we are descended from gods.) They do believe that once, long ago, the gods had lived and ruled among

HATHOR   THOTH   ANUBIS

46

humans but that they were quite separate and did not have human children.

I respect the Egyptian gods, most of whom are represented by animals. Hathor, the goddess of love and beauty, has a cow head and Thoth, the god of wisdom has the head of an ibis. Anubis, the god of the underworld, is a jackal. Isis and Osiris, the most important gods, look more human, even though their son, Horus, has the head of a falcon. Horus was the last of the gods.

ISIS, HORUS & OSIRIS

Egyptians hope to end their human lives as mummies who live on in the underworld. The priests were generous in allowing me to observe how mummies are made; even some animals are mummified, to live in that later world. The process is complicated and takes days, even weeks.

We continued up the Nile to Elephantine. For

MUMMIES WERE PUT INTO WOODEN PORTRAIT CASES

the whole journey, the sailing had been fairly easy, even against the current. The winds at that time

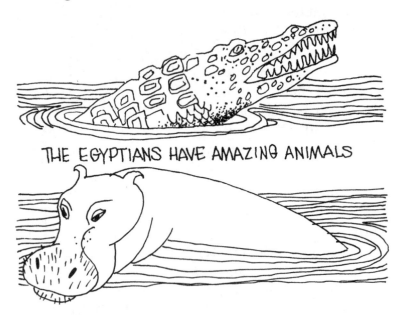

THE EGYPTIANS HAVE AMAZING ANIMALS

of the year blow steadily from north to south, so we sailed with the wind. But the cataracts of the Nile begin at Elephantine and any boats wishing to continue up river must be hoisted to the bank and dragged past each cataract.

I stopped there. Elephantine is the limit of the Persian Empire and I decided not to go on to explore Ethiopia. I would have liked to do that. I have heard that the Ethiopians are the tallest, best-looking people in the world and that they live to be 120 years old.

Cambyses, the Persian king after Cyrus, had tried—and failed—to conquer Ethiopia, but Ethiopian soldiers had come back to Persia, and later served in Xerxes' army. Witnesses told me that they were the handsomest people in the world, that they carried gold-tipped spears and wore leopard or lion skins into battle.

Now we traveled back to the Nile Delta because I wanted to visit Pelusium, the battlefield where the Persian, Cambyses, had defeated Egypt in one great battle. Then I sailed west to the Greek colony of Cyrene, on the bulge of Africa. That was as far west as I went.

There was still more that I wanted to see, so I

went east again, all the way along the Phoenician coast to Tyre where, some 500 years ago, Hiram,

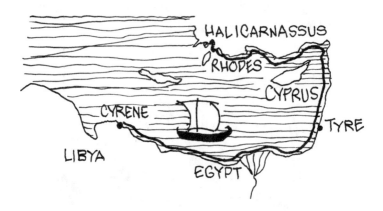

the king, had supplied the cedar to help Solomon build the temple in Jerusalem.

Finally I was ready to go home. I sailed north, past Cyprus and Rhodes, back to Halicarnassus.

In my wanderings I had heard hundreds of stories. I had gathered personal memories of the Persian wars. I had explored seas and rivers, new kinds of plants and strange animals. I had traveled so much that I could describe the geography of much of the known world.

Now I wanted to collect my ideas and adventures and write it all down. Am I a scientist, a geographer or a historian? Maybe I am all of those things.

7

I Write My Histories

So, In My 37th Year, I settled down in Halicarnassus to record my adventures and to share my observations.

We Greeks have known of our past mainly from oral traditions, but I wanted to do something new—to write down, for future generations, what I have discovered about our world today, even if some people aren't going to believe me.

Some things I saw and heard for myself, so I could depend on my own sight and judgment. But

I couldn't go everywhere, so sometimes I relied on what was told to me. I must admit that I couldn't believe all those tales, but I do like a good story so I passed them on. I hope the reader understands which were the things I saw and which were those I only heard about, but some people want to believe anything.

And it also seemed important to tell about the wars of the recent past while there were still eye-witnesses and people who had lived through those times and were eager to talk about them.

So my subject was to be the events and achievements not only of the Greeks, but of mankind. It was to be not only about people and how they behaved, but also about the places where they lived—about geography, climate, plants and animals. I wanted to tell everything I had learned about the known world.

I decided to write my stories as lectures which I could read and recite, to entertain and enlighten audiences of my fellow Greeks.

I began like this:

"Herodotus of Halicarnassus hereby publishes the results of his inquiries, hoping to do two things: to preserve the memory of the past by putting on record the astonishing achievements of both the Greek and non-Greek peoples; more particularly, to show how the two races came in conflict."

Of course I had to start by telling something about the Persians—what they were like, and how

CYRUS

they had come to rule such a great empire. So I began by telling how Cyrus became king of Persia, ruling from the Greek towns on the Aegean Sea to the Persian Gulf.

I tell how he conquers Babylon (I had heard that for myself.) I tell how he got killed in battle, fighting the renowned warriors who live east of the Aral Sea (I had seen those wild people).

Now his son, Cambyses, becomes king of Persia.

I tell how Cambyses conquers Egypt and then

CAMBYSES GOES MAD AND SLAYS THE SACRED APSIS···

went mad and died. (Of course, this was a good place to talk about the marvels of Egypt at length,

DARIUS

so I did. I was sure the Greeks could never hear enough about Egypt.)

Now Darius is chosen king. He builds roads and palaces. He organizes his vast empire into 20 provinces and collects annual tribute from his subjects.

From the Nubians: 2 quarts of gold; 200 logs of ebony; 20 elephant tusks.

54

From the Arabians: 25 and a half tons of frank-
incense.

From India: 360 talents of gold dust.

From the tribes of the Camases: 500 boys.

He collected silver from the sale of fish, and 120,000 measures of grain, and so many talents of gold and silver from his people that he was surely the richest man in the world.

I write how Darius decides to attack the Scythians. He builds a bridge across the Bosporus, so now he is in Europe. Darius conquers Thrace and the Scythians.

(This is a good place for me to talk about Thrace and Scythia and the Scythians' way of life as I saw them in my travels.)

Meanwhile, the Ionian Greeks, my people from the islands in the Aegean Sea, began a revolt.

Now I tell about Athens and the wonderful beginning of Greek democracy. Freedom is an excellent thing. The Athenians, while under the rule of tyrants, were not a whit more valiant than any of their neighbors, but no sooner did they shake off the yoke, than they became decidedly the best and foremost. These things show that while undergoing oppression they let themselves be beaten, but so soon as they got their freedom each man was eager to do the best he could for himself. So fared it now with the Athenians.

THE BATTLE OF MARATHON

PERSIANS

ATHENIANS

THE PERSIANS FLED BACK TO THEIR SHIPS

BAY OF MARATHON

TO ATHENS

490 B.C. I tell about Marathon, where a Persian army of 25,000 men attack 10,000 Greeks. The Greeks win a great victory—a small army of brave men against a huge and confident enemy.

(There's a dramatic story about Pheidippides, (Fi-DIP-i-deez), a Greek at Marathon, who is dispatched to Sparta during the battle,

XERXES

running 26 miles to ask for help. It doesn't come because the Spartans are celebrating a festival.)

Darius dies and his son Xerxes becomes king. Xerxes builds his own bridge across the Hellespont and the Persians cross into Europe.

It gets more and more exciting for us Greeks!

Athens is evacuated. Sparta organizes the Greek cities. All struggles among the Greeks are to stop until the war is over.

Great navies are assembled and wrecked by storms. Great sea battles are fought.

There are a thousand Persian ships. Xerxes sits on a throne overlooking the battles.

When a few Greek deserters were brought into the king's presence, they were asked, "What are the

Greeks doing?" They answered, "They are holding the Olympic games, seeing the athletic sports and the chariot-races."

"And what is the prize for which they contend?" The answer was, "An olive wreath, which is given to the man who wins." Then a courtier exclaimed, "What manner of men are these we fight, who

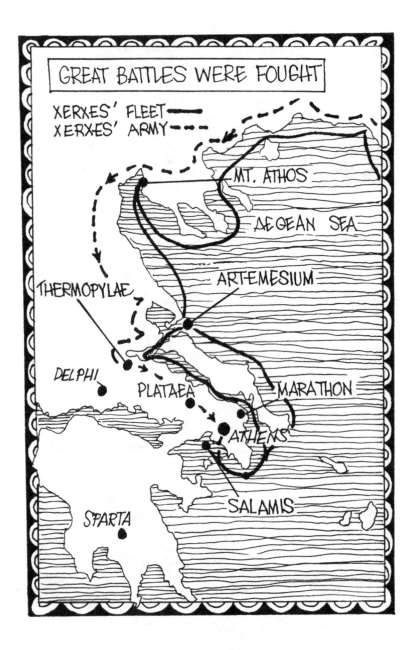

GREAT BATTLES WERE FOUGHT

XERXES' FLEET ——
XERXES' ARMY ----

MT. ATHOS

AEGEAN SEA

ARTEMESIUM

THERMOPYLAE

DELPHI

PLATAEA

MARATHON

ATHENS

SALAMIS

SPARTA

contend with one another, not for money but for honor!"

The fleets and the armies of Athens and Sparta, along with Greek soldiers from other cities, fight back and forth against the Persians.

There are great battles
at Thermopylae,
at Artemesium,
at Salamis,
and Platea.

490-465 B.C.

Finally, the Greeks defeat the Persians.

The Persians were brave warriors in the times of Cyrus, Cambyses and Darius, but Xerxes was cruel and the Persians became spoiled by their luxuries.

Cyrus had said, many years ago, that soft places tend to produce soft men; for the same land cannot yield both wonderful crops and men who are noble and brave in war. Cyrus' words proved true.

I WRITE MY HISTORIES

The Greeks won because they lived in a poor part of the world.

I work hard, along with my scribes, copying and revising my stories until I feel they are ready for the public.

8

To Athens

WHEN MY HISTORIES were transcribed and properly rolled into scrolls for easy reading, I ventured out to recite them to the public.

To my amazement, they were met with indifference and some were even scoffed at. I heard whispers in the audience that I had made everything up; that I hadn't gone to all those places. Instead of being entertained and enlightened, some in my audiences had the audacity to call me a liar!

After several such experiences I decided once again that Halicarnassus was too small and provincial, too self-absorbed to be interested in the larger world. So I packed all my belongings, found a good Phoenician ship to carry me across the Aegean, said goodbye to Halicarnassus forever, and moved to Athens.

We landed at the port of Piraeus and took a fine new road into Athens, which was all I had hoped for. It could certainly be compared to the grand cities I had visited in my travels.

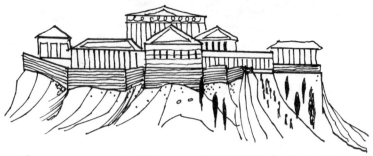

THE ACROPOLIS STOOD HIGH OVER ATHENS

Athens was huge—about 250,000 people lived there. Of these, of course, only 45,000 were male citizens who could vote and take part in the democracy. There were 70,000 slaves and the rest were Greeks from other places, people called metics, who were not citizens. (At the time, this business of citizens and noncitizens didn't seem important to me.)

480 B.C. Thirty years ago Xerxes' general, Mardonius, had wrecked Athens, leaving hardly a stone standing. That was hard to believe, now. Pericles, the ruler, who was also a famous orator and a patron of the arts, was intent on making Athens the most beautiful city in the world.

PERICLES

Such things were going on!

Hippodamus, who was something new—a planner of entire cities—was planning Athens in a scientific way.

HIPPODAMUS

The Acropolis was being rebuilt on the great hill overlooking the city. Phidias, the sculptor, was designing the Parthenon, carving its walls and building enormous statues.

Everywhere I looked, there was art, and the art was created for the people, not the rulers. There were no palaces, only grand public buildings. There were

PHIDIAS

65

SOCRATES

SOPHOCLES

THUCYDIDES

great marketplaces, gyms, and places of assembly. The philosopher, Socrates, was speaking in the streets.

And the theater! There seemed to be a playwright for every theater. Sophocles, the poet and playwright, who became my good friend, wrote wonderful plays. So did Euripides. And Thucydides, who later wrote a history (quite different from mine, I hear), was writing plays, too.

There were other playwrights and musicians and writers and talkers and thinkers and orators and statesmen. I was delighted to become one of their company.

I kept working on my histories. When I thought they were as good as I could make them, I began reciting them at festivals and gatherings, all around Athens. Now, my performances were a great success, which proves how much more intelligent the people of Athens are than the people of Halicarnassus.

My work was so successful that the Athenians rewarded me with a magnificent prize of 60,000 drachmas. That is a lot of money. One drachma is a day's pay for a workman.

So now I was rich and famous. I continued to travel, around mainland Greece and sometimes to the islands. Life was pleasant.

But there was a problem.

I couldn't take part in the democracy. I couldn't

enter politics. I couldn't vote or help make laws or serve on a jury. I wasn't a citizen of Athens and I couldn't become one.

Years ago, Pericles had passed a law that you couldn't be a citizen of Athens unless both your parents had been born in Athens. (He was afraid that Athens would be overrun with Spartans or Corinthians or people from the other Greek states whom he thought were enemies. He thought that if they could become citizens, they might take power from real Athenians.)

I wasn't happy, because to me, a good Greek has to be a citizen—citizenship is his real work. But where could I be a citizen? I certainly didn't want to go back to Halicarnassus.

Athens was eager to start a new colony in Italy and new colonists were promised that they would become citizens there. Athens wanted to settle this new colony in grand style, with important people.

The new city was to be called Thurii.

Hippodamus would plan the colony.

Protagoras, the statesman, would write its laws.

There was a lot of talk and excitement about this new city. Orators described it; poets wrote poems about it and a number of Athenians volunteered to be settlers.

I decided to join them. I was only about 40 years old and I had never been to Italy. So I was off again, to become a citizen of Thurii.

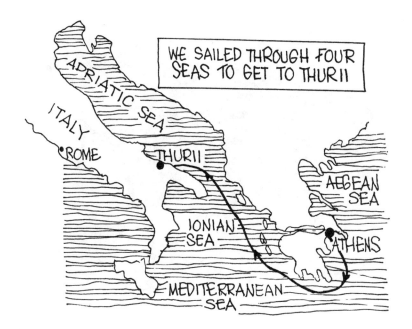

9

To Thurii

THURII WASN'T REALLY a new city—it was built on
the ruins of a famous Greek city called Sybaris,
and Athens was determined to make it fine again.
I didn't go with the first colonists. By the time I
got there, Hippodamus had laid out the city and
it was growing and thriving.

In Thurii, I kept working on my histories, reciting them and adding new ideas as I thought back
over my travels and my interviews. Thurii was

becoming bigger, more prosperous and more so-
phisticated, so there were plays, lectures and visit-
ing dignitaries to keep me busy. And I did quite a
lot of traveling around the mainland and the islands. About ten years passed pleasantly for me.

Then I began to hear so much about what was
going on in Athens that I decided to go back for a
visit. The city had been entirely rebuilt!

The Parthenon was finished—it was a grand
spectacle of gleaming white marble with brightly
painted, carved friezes.

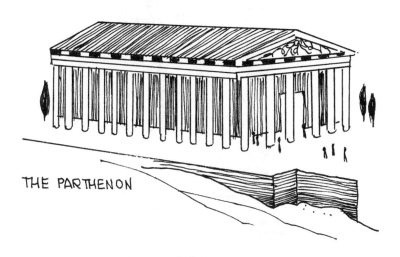

THE PARTHENON

Phidias' giant gold and ivory statue of Athena
was in place. She was so tall that when I stood
beside her and looked up, her head almost van-
ished above me.

The city was splendid, but still there was an uneasiness. War with Sparta was in the air.

I had been in Athens for about a year when a horrible plague broke out, sweeping the city. Disease was everywhere—among the rich, among the

poor, even in the barracks. A third or more of the population died—the strong and healthy as well as the old and poor.

I was glad to have a place to flee to, so I sailed back to Thurii.

And here I stay, to keep writing, and no doubt traveling, until the end of my days. I won't be bored! I am still thinking about the people, things and places I have yet to see.

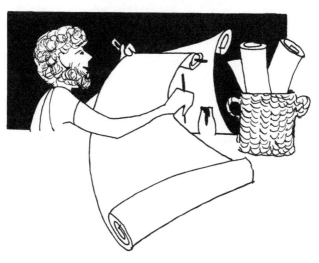

Epilogue

Some people say that Herodotus died in the plague in Athens, but most historians think he went back to Thurii, continued to revise his histories and that he lived well into his old age.

Another historian reported seeing his tomb in Thurii, right there in the marketplace.

Even the greatest traveler of his time has to rest at last.

Jeanne Bendick

Note: Most historians put his death at around 424 B.C.

Names of Places, Ancient and Modern

These are the modern geographical names we have used in the book, followed by their names in Herodotus' time.

Arabian Gulf (The Red Sea): The Erythraean

Azov Sea: Lake Maeotis

Bug River: The Hypanis

Black Sea: The Euxine

Bosporus: The Bosporus

Danube River: The Ister

Dnieper River: The Tyras

Don River: The Tanais

Marmara Sea: The Propontis

In the case of the following three names we retained the usage of Herodotus' time. Here we list the ancient usage first, the modern name second.

The Pillars of Hercules: The Strait of Gibraltar

The Hellespont: The Dardanelles

The Tin Islands: The British Isles

Brief Glossary of Persons Mentioned

Aesop (EE-sop)—Greek slave, writer of *The Fables*

Anaximander (An-ax-i-MAN-der) of Miletus—early Greek geographer

Artemisia (Ar-tuh-MIH-zha)—woman ruler of Halicarnassus, and ship commander for the Persians

Cambyses (Cam-BYE-seez)—Persian Emperor, son of Cyrus

Cyrus (SYE-rus) the Great—founder of the Persian Empire

Darius (Duh-RYE-us)—Persian emperor after Cambyses

Euripides (you-RIP-i-deez)—Greek dramatist

Hecataeus (Ha-KAY-tee-us) of Miletus—Greek geographer just before Herodotus

Hippodamus (Hippo-DAY-mus) of Miletus—Greek planner of cities

Jason and Medea (Mih-DEE-ah)—Figures in Greek mythology. Jason with a band of heroes (the Argonauts), and the king of Colchis' daughter

Medea, got back the Golden Fleece, originally stolen from Jason's father.

Lygdamis (LIG-dah-miss)—tyrant of Halicarnassus, grandson of Artemisia

Mardonius (Mar-DOH-nee-us)—Persian army commander under Xerxes

Pericles (PAIR-ih-kleez)—Greek statesman and ruler of Athens

Phidias (FID-ee-us)—Greek sculptor and designer of the Parthenon

Protagoras (Pro-TAG-or-us)—Greek philosopher and statesman

Pythagoras (Pith-AG-or-us)—of Samos, Greek philosopher and mathematician

Socrates (SOCK-rah-teez)—Greek philosopher

Sophocles (SOFF-oh-cleez)—Greek dramatist

Thucydides (Thoo-SID-ih-deez)—Greek historian, younger than Herodotus

Xerxes (ZERK-seez)—Persian Emperor, son of Darius

Measurements

Units of Length:
A finger was 3/4 inch
A foot was 16 fingers
1 1/2 feet was a cubit
6 feet was a fathom
100 feet was a plethron
600 feet was a stade
1/8 of a mile (220 yards) was a furlong
3 1/2 miles was a parasang

Units of Measure:
A drachma weighed .15 oz.
A mina (100 drachma) weighed 15 oz.
A talent weighed 57 pounds
An amphora held liquid: 39.39 liters; 10.4 US gallons

The unit of money was the obol. 6 obols made a drachma

About the Author

Jeanne Bendick, a graduate of Parsons School of Design, is the author and illustrator of many books, primarily in the field of science. Her work has always been distinguished by her remarkable ability to express complex concepts in simple language, and to make difficult subjects interesting and comprehensible to the general reader. Among her many books are *Archimedes and the Door of Science, Galen and the Gateway to Medicine, Along Came Galileo,* and *Egyptian Tombs.*